The Adventures of Amilya Rose

Disappearance

Chavonne D. Stewart

Dogwood Farms Publications

Cover Art by Jasmine Mills
Illustrations by Jasmine Mills
Edited by Lisa J. Lickel
Co-Edited by Rachel McDermott

This book is a work of fiction and any resemblance to persons, living or dead, or places, events, or locales is purely coincidental. The characters are the product of the author's imagination and used fictitiously.

Scripture taken from the NASB © Copyright 1960, 1962, 1963, 1968, 1971, 1972, 1973, 1975, 1977 by the Lockman Foundation. Used with permission.

Published by Dogwood Farms Publications
Juvenile Fiction – Chapter Book – Social Issues/Peer Pressure

Library of Congress Control Number: 2015906367
Hardcover ISBN 978-0-9863128-5-4
Paper ISBN 978-0-9863128-3-0
Electronic book ISBN978-0-9863128-4-7
Published in the United States of America
Contact info: PO Box 2598 Acworth, GA 30101
www.ChavonneStewart.com

Amilya Rose Patterson is a witty eight-year-old with lots of personality. With her "can do" attitude and dynamic brainpower she is very creative and has a vivid imagination. As a result of her imagination, Amilya is determined to set out on a new adventure during summer vacation. This time she decides to add a disappearing act to her list of adventures. In the end, what lesson will she learn?

So, friends, come along, join Amilya Rose on her adventure.

Acknowledgements

For I am confident of this very thing, that He who began a good work in you will perfect it until the day of Christ Jesus.

Philippians 1:6 NASB

First, I would like to thank God for being my source and strength. To my family and close friends, thank you for all your love, support and encouragement. Special dedication to the best grandparents in the world...I love and miss you...Robert and LueVert Grant: the memories you made are everlasting.

i

Table of Contents

Chapter One
Last Day of School

My alarm clock chimes like a bird, and I sit straight up in my bed. I say, "It's Friday, the last day of school!" and I hop out of bed so fast that I tumble to the floor.

The fall didn't hurt me, so I giggle. I'm excited because I get to spend the summer with the best grandparents in the world: Big Daddy and Big Momma. But before my summer vacation begins, I have to make it through the day. Luckily, there is no more classwork left to do. Wyndell Elementary has been having field days all week!

My parents are always telling my teachers that I am mischievous, but most of my teachers have concluded that I am just adventurous. I usually do something out of the ordinary daily, but I guess I have been waiting for school to get out before I attempt any more adventures.

During my last adventure, I lied so much that even I could not recognize the truth. I didn't want to get into any more trouble at school, so I haven't been on an adventure in a long time. The only good thing that came out of my last adventure is that I am now allowed to walk to the daycare after school as long as Mom follows me in the car. It's a bit ridiculous, but I am glad I get to walk more.

I can only imagine what type of trouble I am going to get into this summer because I am long overdue for some excitement!

I start preparing for my day by making my bed. Each class at Wyndell gets their own field day, and today is the third grade's field day. I am going to wear my blue jean shorts, a t-shirt that says Wyndell Elementary Wildcats, and a pair of sneakers. I get completely dressed for breakfast, then I walk towards my little brother's room.

Caleb is getting ready for daycare. It's hard to believe Caleb will be going to school with me next year. He will be in kindergarten.

"Good morning, Caleb," I say.

"Hi, Millie," says Caleb. "Guess what?"

"What?" I say.

"I lost another tooth this morning."

"Really? How many so far and where?" I ask.

"Both of my front teeth! I'm growing up," Caleb says.

"Yes, you are."

In the background I hear our mom calling.

"Caleb and Amilya, time for breakfast!"

"Okay!" we say.

As we enter the kitchen, I see that Daddy is already seated. He took off work today so he can come to my field day. A lot of parents volunteer to help with field day.

"Good morning, Mommy and Daddy," Caleb and I say.

"Good morning, kiddos," says Daddy.

"Mommy, what's for breakfast?" I ask.

"We are having pancakes, eggs and sausage."

"Yummy!" I respond.

Caleb loves pancakes. "Yay!" he says. Daddy is reading the morning paper while we are waiting for Mom to serve breakfast, and Caleb sits beside him. "What section of the paper are you reading?"

"Well, I am reading the sports section now. It's baseball season."

Daddy always takes us to games, and Caleb really enjoys them. Caleb likes baseball, so he plays T-ball. I also like baseball, but I play soccer, and I am a cheerleader during football season.

"Daddy?" asks Caleb.

"Yes?"

"Who won the baseball game last night?"

"Our Atlanta Braves won. They beat the Los Angeles Dodgers by four points."

"OO-ooh, that sounds like a great game!" says Caleb. "When are we going to another game?"

"Soon, probably next week."

"I can't wait, Daddy! I hope I'll catch a ball."

"I hope so, too, Son."

As Caleb and Daddy have their conversation, I help Mom set the table. We bring all the food to the table in serving dishes, and Daddy says a prayer over the food before we pass the dishes. I love butter pecan syrup on my pancakes, but Caleb puts strawberry syrup on his.

As we eat, it is so quiet that you could hear a pin drop. We are enjoying our food. Next thing I know, Mommy is speaking to Caleb and me.

"All right, kiddos, time for school and daycare. Be sure you grab your book bags."

"Yes, ma'am," we say.

"Caleb?" she says.

"Yes?"

"Grab your lunch."

"Oh, yeah. Why doesn't Amilya need a lunch today?" Caleb doesn't know my school is having field day. The PTA provides the food for the kids during this week.

"Caleb, none of your business, just do as you are told," I say.

"OOO-kay!" says Caleb.

"Do you have your book bags?" Mom asks us.

"Yes, ma'am, we do," I say.

Caleb grabs his toys, and I pick the visor with my name on the front.

"Amilya, did you put on sunscreen?" says Mommy.

"Yes, ma'am."

Everybody gets in the car, and Dad pulls out of the garage. Caleb and I started singing, but this time we make up a tune. Our parents laugh joyously.

Dad drops Caleb off at daycare first, then we head to good old Wyndell Elementary. When we arrive, we head towards Ms. Honeycutt's room.

Mr. Humphries is standing at the door, so we

greet him.

"Good morning Mr. Humphries," Mommy and Daddy say.

"Good morning, Mr. and Mrs. Patterson, and Amilya Rose."

"Morning," I say.

"Great weather for field day," says Daddy.

"Yes, it is," says Mr. Humphries. "Amilya, what events are you going to participate in today?"

"I am going to do tug-of-war, the fifty-yard dash, and the sack race." I am really excited.

"Sounds wonderful. Well, be on your best behavior. Don't do anything I wouldn't do."

"Yes, sir."

Finally, we enter Ms. Honeycutt's room, and I go straight to my desk. There are lot of kids and parents swarming around. My classroom is housing all the water for the day, as well as the sacks for the sack race.

Next thing I know, all the students are seated at their desks. Ms. Honeycutt asks that we all quiet down, then she tells the parents what they must do to set up for the day.

The parents begin to move all the supplies outside. After the Pledge of Allegiance, Ms. Honeycutt takes the roll. This time, however, she hands us each name badges, and she starts to review the rules we must follow.

As Ms. Honeycutt talks about the rules, I start to daydream. Don't get me wrong, I am excited about field day. However, I am more excited about what is going to happen after school: summer vacation! Hooray!

Summer vacation is my favorite time of the year. First, I get to wear shorts, t-shirts, and sandals or sneakers all the time. I don't like wearing sweaters or coats. I get to go swimming, and I visit the zoo, aquarium, and amusement parks.

Second, I get to spend the summer days with my grandparents. My cousins and I call them Big Momma and Big Daddy. I love them so much, and we always have fun. We play games like UNO or Old Maid, and we sit on the front porch watching TV. We laugh, talk and tell jokes, and dance.

Third, I get to play with all the neighborhood kids at the playground, especially my best friends forever: Leah, Jackson, and Christie. We also like to ride our bikes around the neighborhood together.

My daydream is interrupted by Ms. Honeycutt calling my name.

"Amilya? Amilya Rose," says Ms. Honeycutt.

"Yes, ma'am," I say.

"Please get in line," says Ms. Honeycutt.

As I am slowly drifting back from my daydream to reality, I notice that Ms. Honeycutt has told the class to line up single file. My class heads out to the field and joins the other five third grade classes at Wyndell. Let the games begin!

I see the parents preparing hotdogs, hamburgers, chips, baked beans, cookies, cupcakes, water, Gatorade, and soda for lunch. Our parents really know how to take care of us!

Time seems to move by pretty swiftly because I don't have access to a clock while I am outside. The first event is the hundred-yard dash, and before I know it, it's time for the fifty-yard dash. I do my best and win first place!

Eventually, the last event of the day is here: the tug of war. The last two classes to compete are Ms. Honeycutt's Hornets and Mr. Blake's Bears. As I line up with my class, I hope the bell will ring soon.

I must have looked distracted because Ms. Honeycutt asked me, "Amilya Rose, are you ready?"

"Yes, ma'am," I say.

"Are you sure you want to compete?"

"Of course I do! This is my favorite event. Hornets Rule!"

"Growling! Screaming! Screeching! Honeycutt Hornets and Blake Bears do," the kids all chant.

Christie and Jackson are on the Blake Bears team. Leah, my other bestie, is on the Honeycutt Hornets team with me. I hear the parents, teachers, and other classes yelling and cheering as we tug-tug away. Finally, the Bears come tumbling down.

"Hooray! We win!" my team shouts.

Ms. Honeycutt's class rules!

Now field day is over, and a brief moment of sadness comes over me as we pack up everything and head back to our classrooms. As eager as I am for summer break to begin, I did enjoy my field day.

Once we get back into the room, we clean out our desks. We have about forty-five minutes to go.

"Great job, class," says Ms. Honeycutt.

"Thank you, Ms. Honeycutt," we say.

"I really enjoyed being your teacher this

year. I hope you all will have a wonderful summer." Ms. Honeycutt looks at the clock and says, "You can talk quietly and sign each other's yearbooks for the last few minutes."

"Thank you, Ms. Honeycutt! We love you," we say.

I make sure everyone signs my yearbook, then I pack my book bag and go over to Leah. We start talking about our summer plans.

"Leah, what are you going to do tomorrow?" I ask. "You know, it's our first day away from school."

"My parents are taking us to the movies, then I will probably play outside," says Leah.

"Sounds fun," I respond.

"Anything I get to do will be fun as long as I don't have to do any homework," says Leah.

"I know what you mean."

"Will you get to spend time with your grandparents for the summer, too?" I ask.

"Yes. Then we can go on an adventure," says Leah.

"Oooooh, yes, I love adventures," I say.

I can feel my stomach swirling. I know the bell is going to ring soon, and summer vacation will be here. I will be free!

As much as I love walking to the daycare, I need to move quickly today. I will just get in the car and go because Ms. Ruffles at Cuddle Time has a big treat for us. I really don't want to miss it!

Before I know it, I look up at the clock, and see there is one minute to go before the bell. Ten, nine, and eight, seven, six, five, four, three, two, one....Ding Dong Ding goes the school bell!

I am officially out of the third grade. No more homework, except for summer reading. But, most importantly, Caleb and I get to spend time with our grandparents!

Chapter Two
Summer Vacation

There are a couple of days before we go to our grandparents' house, so Caleb and I start our summer vacation at the state fair on Saturday. We enjoy amusement parks and love to hear the laughter and screams of the kids.

Caleb and I play ski ball and basketball, and we ride every ride possible. We eat cotton candy, hotdogs, funnel cakes, and popcorn. However, even though I am having a blast at the state fair, I am still thinking about going to my grandparents' house. Caleb and I spend the majority of our summer days at their home, and I can't wait to go!

"Millie...Millie...Mil—lie!" says Caleb.

"What?" I must have been daydreaming again.

Caleb frowns. "I was trying to ask you a question, but you were ignoring me."

"I'm sorry, what's your question?"

"Well, are you going to answer or ignore me?"

I patiently say, "I'll answer you this time."

"What were you thinking about?"

I don't like it when people ask what I was thinking. "None of your business, Caleb. Is that what you wanted to ask me?"

"No, I just wanted know if we can ride the bumper cars again."

"Oh. Um, I guess so."

"I'll race you! On your mark, get set, go."

As we start to run, I hear my mom yell, "Hold it!"

We stop in our tracks and turn around.

"Kids, it's time to go home," says Mom.

"Oh no! Mom, please, please can we ride the bumper cars one more time?" Caleb asks.

"We've have been here since ten o'clock this morning, and it's time to go," says Dad.

Caleb starts to cry, but I don't really care about riding the bumper cars again. My focus is on going to my Big Daddy and Big Momma's house! I walk to the car in a daze because I am thinking about all the exciting things I could do this summer. I know an adventure is in the making, but I don't have a plan yet.

My family and I get into the car, and Caleb cries himself to sleep during the ride home. Though summertime adventures are swirling through my head, I'm tired after spending eight hours at the state fair. I soon start to drift a little as well.

When we arrive home, my mom says it's bath time then bedtime. The house is quiet when I go to bed, but I can hear the neighborhood dogs howling at the moon. Before long, everyone is asleep.

Sunday is church day, then I get to see Big Momma and Big Daddy on Monday!

* * * *

I lay in bed on Monday morning, listening to the clock in the hallway ticking. Then my alarm finally goes off, and I quickly hop out of bed. It's time to go to Big Momma's house!

Oh my, I have to decide what to wear. One of the many great things about summer is that I can wear shorts, t-shirts and sandals every day, but I keep my sneakers close by just in case.

If you're wondering why I said "just in case," it's because I have to be prepared for my adventures at all times.

I run to the kitchen immediately after getting dressed. My mom is not in the kitchen yet, but since I only want cereal this morning, I can serve myself. I get my own bowl, spoon, milk, and cereal and set them on the table.

Caleb comes into the kitchen. "Good morning, Millie."

"Morning! How did you sleep?"

"Pretty good. I had a dream that I got a dog for my birthday."

"Oh, really?" I try not to roll my eyes because Caleb has been asking for a dog since he learned how to speak. I don't know if he ever will get one, but I say, "Hopefully, you will get your dog this year."

Mom and Dad join us, and Mom makes Caleb some oatmeal. I eat my breakfast quickly, but Caleb plays with his oatmeal while Mom packs snacks to take with us.

"Kids, your dad will drop you off this morning," says Mom.

"Okay," we say. I really don't care who takes me to my grandparents as long as I get there.

When Caleb is finished with breakfast, we grab our bags and head to the car. My dad waits until we are buckled in, then he cranks the car and pulls out of the garage. Caleb and I start to sing, and Daddy joins in.

As we cruise down the road, I look forward to the yummy treats our grandparents will have for us this summer: frosted flakes, watermelon, ribs, chicken, BLTs, and chocolate milk.

I smile as I think about my grandparents. Big Daddy is very tall and wide, he has mixed gray hair, and he loves to smile. He usually wears blue jeans and a plaid shirt. He drives a big, green, old-fashioned car that is always loaded with tools and goodies. Big Momma is shorter than Big Daddy. She has soft, long gray hair and pretty brown eyes. I love to hear her laugh because it makes me want to laugh, too.

Also, my great-great aunt Rose lives with my grandparents. I was partially named after her. Caleb and I stay away from her, though, because we think she is kind of creepy. She is really old, and she usually stays in the front bedroom of the house. If she walks around, she just shuffles along with her walker.

Aunt Rose always wears wigs that look like a dead animal, and she makes weird noises. Big Momma says she is just taking deep breaths so she can talk, but I think her deep breaths would scare away the chickens if we had some.

My grandparents' house is red brick with a huge screened front porch, and it is located at the corner of Boulevard Drive and Third Avenue. Out front there is a long brick path that leads to the front door, and it has grass on each side.

In the backyard, Big Daddy built three small white houses. Two are used to store his tools, but the third is where my cousins and I go to hang out. We like to listen to music, dance, laugh, and eat Popsicles.

There are several great climbing trees in the front and back yards, but I love the huge pecan tree that is located on the side of the house. I have learned that pecan trees are very peculiar because pecans only grow every other year. I hope this year I will be able to climb the tree and pick some.

Whenever I think about my grandparents' home, I also think about the rest of the neighborhood. No matter what day of the week it is, we never know what to expect in my grandparents' neighborhood because there are some wacky neighbors that live nearby.

For instance, there is Mrs. Peabody. She is a short, old white lady who lives alone with two big dogs. I believe they are Dobermans. Her hair is all white, and it looks like a big fluffy cotton ball. She wears very thick glasses, and she owns a big car like an Oldsmobile. I think she loves pink because every time I see her she is wearing something pink.

Every time Mrs. Peabody comes out her front door with her

dogs, all the kids run for safety. She is supposedly walking the dogs, but it doesn't look that way to me. The dogs pull away from her so much that it's like they are walking Mrs. Peabody.

Then there are the Crumbs, who live across the street from Big Momma's house. They have a white house with a front porch and a white picket fence. Mr. Crumb drives an old blue Ford pickup truck. He is very tall, and he always wears overalls. Mrs. Crumb makes the best banana pudding. She has long dark hair, and just like Mr. Crumb, she wears overalls. Their grandkids, Christie and Matt, come to visit every summer. Christie is one of my best friends from school, and I'm glad I get to spend time with her.

Ms. Tomlin is another neighbor. She always makes sure we are doing what's right, so I call her the neighborhood Robocop for kids. If we do anything wrong, she will be the one to tell on us. She is a thin, older black lady. She loves to work in her yard and plant flowers. Actually, she dabbles in everybody's yards on the street side.

The Fords live up the street, and I think Mrs. Ford is a busybody. She knows everyone's business, but of course no one really knows hers. Her house is olive green with black shutters. Her grandson, Timothy, lives with her all the time. My school friend, Jackson, is friends with Timothy, and sometimes he will come spend time with Timothy during the summer.

One thing I love about my grandparents' neighborhood is its huge sidewalk. There is plenty of room for kids to ride bikes, walk, and play safely.

All of a sudden, I hear car doors opening, and my daydream comes to an end.

As Caleb and I get out of the car, Dad gives us each a hug and kiss on the cheek. We say good-bye, and Dad drives away. I look up towards Mrs. Peabody's house, and I notice a huge moving van about six houses up from my grandparents. I widen my eyes with excitement because I know in my heart what my next adventure will be: visiting the new neighbors!

I start to make plans as I walk up the path to Big Momma's house.

Chapter Three
The Adventure

"Hello, my babies," says Big Momma when she opens the front door.

I am so excited! "Hi, Big Momma! How are you?"

"I am blessed, baby."

Caleb reaches to give her a hug, but he cannot speak because his mouth is full of candy.

"So, tell me how well you did in school, Amilya Rose," says Big Momma.

"I got four A's and one B."

"Good job, young lady! I am so proud of you. What class did you get the B in?"

I scrunch up my face. "Science. I'm not a real big fan." I wonder if Big Momma knows who the new neighbors are, so I ask, "Who is moving into the old Peterson house?"

"I'm not sure, baby. Why do you ask?"

"Just curious, Big Momma. I saw a big moving truck in the yard."

"You know you are not allowed to go that far from our home."

"Yes, ma'am, I know."

"Amilya, I want you to be on the best behavior this summer. Don't do any disappearing acts or create any plots that can cause harm."

"Ummmm-hmmm."

I will do my best to obey, but I am so curious about our new neighbors! I wonder if they have any kids. Caleb and I will be over here daily, so I have to know who is moving in.

I decide that before this day ends, I will have completed my adventure. I need to plan wisely because I have to get away from Caleb. He would tell Big Momma if he saw me going to the new neighbor's house.

Caleb and I go into the den, and we put our book bags in the corner. The phone rings and Big Momma answers. She isn't on the phone long.

"Babies, are you all hungry?" Big Momma asks. She loves to feed us even when we are not hungry.

"No, ma'am," we say.

"Okay, I can microwave your food when you are ready."

"Where is Big Daddy?" Caleb asks.

"He is at work right now. He'll be home later on," Big Momma says.

"Big Momma, can I go outside and play?" I ask.

"As long as you take your brother."

Aw, man. "Do I have to?" I really don't want to take Caleb. I am ready to explore!

"Amilya Rose, do you hear me?" Big Momma says.

"Yes, ma'am."

"You know your brother likes to play. You can't go out if you don't take him with you."

"But, Big Momma—"

"No buts, young lady. If you continue to pester me, you all will have to play inside the house."

Fine, I will take Caleb. "Yes, ma'am. Come on, Caleb, and leave your toy cars. You'll cry if you lose them."

"Millie, I won't cry, I'm a big boy now."

"Yeah, sure you are." I chuckle to myself.

I think about how can I get rid of Caleb long enough to go see what's going on up at the big white house on the hill. Caleb has friends in the neighborhood. Aidan and Andrew are twins, and they love climbing trees and picking up the most peculiar bugs.

"Let's go and see if Aidan and Andrew are here," I say.

We walk out the front door. Caleb grabs his scooter from the garage, and we go down the walkway to the main sidewalk. Aidan and Andrew live down the street about six houses down from Big Momma. I start to walk in that direction, and Caleb rides next to me, whistling.

I think about the new neighbors as I walk. The Petersons are an older couple who used to live in the big white house up the

17

street, but they moved away a year ago. Their granddaughter, Tammi, is my age. Tammi would always spend the summers with her grandparents, and we would play together all the time. I really miss her!

As I think about Tammi, I hope Caleb will get distracted so I can slip away.

We reach Aidan and Andrew's house.

"We're here," Caleb says.

"Okay, go and ring the doorbell," I say.

Caleb drops his scooter and runs up to the front door. He rings the doorbell, and Aiden answers the door.

Caleb says, "Hi, Aidan. Can you and Andrew come out and play?"

"Just a second, let me ask my mom," said Aidan.

I am in my own little world as I stare up the road. My heart is pounding because I am anxious to move forward with my adventure. I start to formulate a plan to get away from Caleb.

I can't walk directly in front of Big Momma's house because Big Momma might be seated on the front porch. I will be in trouble if she sees me without Caleb. I have to sneak through the backyard, but first, I have to cut behind Mr. Wiggins' house. Then I will cross Big Momma's backyard. The final obstacle is the fence that connects Big Momma's house to Mrs. Peabody's.

As I am thinking, I hear laughter. Caleb, Aidan, and Andrew are playing baseball. Caleb forgot I was even there, so now is my chance to get away!

I walk swiftly down the sidewalk to Mr. Wiggins' house, hoping he isn't home. I look around the corner because I know he drives an old burgundy Lincoln. The car is not in the yard.

Away I go!

I walk diagonally through Mr. Wiggins' yard to Big Momma's

backyard. Big Momma's eyesight isn't all that good, so I don't think she will see me if she looks out the window. I jump the fence into Mrs. Peabody's yard, and I am glad I have on my shorts.

I hear Mrs. Peabody's dogs barking as I scurry past her back door, but they are inside so I am okay. I slip around the side of Mrs. Peabody's house and walk up to the sidewalk.

Nothing can stop me now!

I walk up the sidewalk and to my surprise, none of Big Momma's neighbors are on their front porches. Trouble would have come knocking if I were caught. I start to skip towards the big white house.

A lady comes out the front door when I reach the front driveway. I recognize her as Tammi's aunt, but I don't remember her name.

I walk up to Tammi's aunt and introduce myself. "Hi, my name is Amilya Rose."

"Well, hello, Amilya Rose," Tammi's aunt responds.

"I remember seeing you here before when I was playing with Tammi, but I don't know your name."

"My name is Sylvia. I'm Tammi's aunt. Actually, Tammi is here visiting me."

Yay! I giggle to myself because I didn't expect to see Tammi. "Can I come in to play with her?" I ask.

"Does your grandmother know you are up here?" Aunt Sylvia asks.

I am shocked. How does she know Big Momma?

"Yes, ma'am," I say.

Uh-oh! I lied again. I can't seem to learn my lesson when it comes to lying. I think I am always afraid to hear "no" when I want to be adventurous. Lucky for me, today's adventure just became a two-part series!

I may have lied, but the adventure must go on. I enter the house and walk into the family room. Tammi is sitting on the floor playing with her dolls.

"Hi, Tammi," I say.

Tammi leaps up and gives me a hug. "Amilya Rose, it's been a long time."

"I know! Will you be spending the summer here or going back home?"

"I'm staying here all summer," Tammi responds.

"Awesome!"

"What would you like to play?"

"We can play dress up like we used to. Do you think your aunt would mind us playing in her clothes?" I ask.

I didn't realize that Aunt Sylvia was standing right behind us. Tammi and I hear her giggle, so we turn and look.

"Well, little ladies, I don't mind you all playing dress up," Aunt Sylvia says. "Just be sure not play in my formal gowns."

"Yes, ma'am," we respond.

Tammi and I walk up the stairs and enter her aunt's huge bedroom. The walk-in closet is full of clothes, and Tammi and I have a field day as we dig through them. We laugh and talk about school. I completely forget about Caleb, the time, and what Big Momma told me.

Tammi and I dress like little old ladies, and Aunt Sylvia brings us tea, sandwiches, and cupcakes. As we sip tea we speak with accents. Tammi does a French accent and I do a British accent.

We laugh and talk some more, then we play Old Maid. When we're finished, we change our looks to models. We decide to do a fashion show for Aunt Sylvia.

I don't pay attention to the time until Aunt Sylvia mentions it. "Amilya Rose, shouldn't you be going home?" she asks.

"Big Momma is okay with me being up here," I say.

Next thing I know, Aunt Sylvia has fallen asleep. Tammi and I play some more, and we play and laugh so hard that we also fall asleep.

When Aunt Sylvia wakes up from her nap, she wakes us up as well. "Amilya Rose, it's time for you to go home," she says.

"Yes, ma'am," I say.

"You have been here for at least four hours, and I know your Big Momma must be worried."

"I doubt she is worried. She knows I am out playing."

"You can come back tomorrow to play with Tammi," says Aunt Sylvia.

Tammi and I change into our clothes and put Aunt Sylvia's clothes back in their rightful places in the closet. Tammi fixes the bed, and I grab the tray with the teacups. We go back downstairs.

By the time we get downstairs, Aunt Sylvia is sitting on the porch.

Tammi and I step out on the porch, and I say, "Thank you for allowing me to play with Tammi today, Aunt Sylvia. I really enjoyed myself."

"You're welcome," says Aunt Sylvia. "I enjoyed seeing you again, Amilya Rose."

Before I can tell Tammi good-bye, I notice a lot of police cars down the road. This community has Neighborhood Watch, so the police patrol the area a lot.

"I wonder what's happened," says Aunt Sylvia.

I didn't know what happened, and right then I didn't really care. Police swarming the neighborhood couldn't involve me.

Tammi and I shrug our shoulders and say, "We don't know."

"Amilya Rose, you'd better get back home, just in case," says Aunt Sylvia.

"Okay," I say. "Bye, Tammi, see you tomorrow."

Tammi waves at me as I walk away. "Bye-bye!" she says.

My adventure has come to an end. I had an awesome time, and no one got hurt or in trouble. I guess I'd better go join Caleb at Aidan and Andrew's house. If I can get there without Big Momma seeing me, I'll be home free!

Chapter Four
The Brick Wall

I notice that Aunt Sylvia is in the yard watching me as I walk away. I guess she wants to make sure I make it home safely.

I whistle and skip as I head down the sidewalk. I had so much fun today! I am glad Tammi will be able to stay for the summer. Now all I need is for Jackson, Leah, and Christie to come over, and my summer playtime will be complete.

I am not paying attention to what I am doing, and I forget to cut through the backyards to get to back to Caleb. I realize my mistake too late: I am almost past Mrs. Peabody's house.

I stop in my tracks and hope that Big Momma is not sitting on her front porch. Even though she can't see very well, she would surely be able to notice me coming. I find myself moving forward again, but this time I take smaller steps. There is a brick wall that separates Big Momma's front yard from Mrs. Peabody's, and Big Momma plants flowers in the planters on the wall every year.

I start to tip-tip toe, and I wonder if Big Momma has the shades pulled down on the porch to keep the sun out. Just as I pass the brick wall, I run into Big Momma. She was waiting for me, but how did she know I was going to come down that way?

Big Momma is not happy at all. She has a stern look on her face and I can almost see smoke coming out of her ears. I pause before I speak. "Hi, Big Momma," I say.

Nothing but silence.

"Are you watering your flowers?" I ask.

Once again, nothing but silence. I think I can distract her by asking questions. I need to get my story together.

"Amilya Rose," she finally says. Her voice is so deep it's like she's growling at me. Right now, she is not the sweet, loving grandmother that I know. "Where have you been?" she asks.

I am determined not to give myself away. "I am playing hide and seek with Caleb," I say.

Oh my, here I go again. I really need to stop lying!

"Really," says Big Momma. "Where have you been hiding? Caleb came home about three hours ago."

A shock wave goes up my spine. What do I do now? Caleb has ruined my adventure by coming home early. "Big Momma, are you sure Caleb is home?" I ask.

"Amilya Rose Patterson, your brother is climbing the pecan tree next to the house," says Big Momma. She turns completely around and points to the pecan tree. I am surprised at how fast she moved because she usually moves slowly.

I know I am in deep, deep trouble now because Big Momma has called me by my full name. I look at the pecan tree, and sure enough, there is Caleb swinging from one of the tree limbs. He is getting away with swinging from a limb because Big Momma is focused on me. Caleb never gets caught!

"Young lady, I am going to ask you one more time. Where have you been? You better not lie to me again."

At this point, I don't know what to say. I feel like I have to tell another lie because I don't want to say what I was actually doing. "Big Momma, you know Andrew and Aidan's neighbors, the Bakers? I was playing with Missy, their daughter."

"Amilya, you are lying," Big Momma says. "Since you are choosing to lie, you are grounded."

"But, Big Momma, I am telling you the truth," I say.

"NO! You are not," Big Momma says. "Now go have a seat on the front porch."

My head slumps downward and my eyes fill with tears. She

has never spoken to me that way before, and her words pierce my heart. I just wanted to know who was moving into the house up the street!

When I open the door to the front porch, Big Daddy is sitting there with a police officer. I take a deep breath, hoping that the officer is a distraction for Big Daddy. I don't feel like being asked more questions.

"Hi, Big Daddy," I say. I run to him and gave him a big hug.

He hugs back and kisses me on the cheek, but he says, "Amilya, be quiet and have a seat."

Oh my, this is not how Big Daddy normally greets me. He always greets me with a bear hug and a smile. His face is almost scary, and I know I am in double trouble.

The officer looks at me as he talks with Big Daddy. "She looks safe. I don't think any harm has come to her."

I widen my eyes. They called the police on me! But why?

"Amilya, why are you looking at the officer that way?" Big Daddy asks.

"I don't understand why the police are here," I say.

"Amilya Rose Patterson, your Big Momma could not find you," says Big Daddy. "You disappeared, so I called the police to report you missing."

I am stunned, and no words come out of my mouth.

The officer gets up to leave, and he speaks to me. "Good bye, Amilya Rose. You stay out of trouble, you hear?"

I don't really know what to say. "Have a nice day, officer."

As the police officer walks away, Big Momma walks up to the porch with Caleb right behind her. Big Momma asks Caleb to go into the den to watch TV. Caleb obeys reluctantly, and I know he wants to hear what will happen to me.

Big Momma sits in her favorite chair in the corner, and I

watch the TV they keep out here. I hope that no one will say anything, but my hopes are quickly crushed.

Big Momma turns off the television and the questions begin. She just comes out with it: "Amilya, you went to the white house up the street, didn't you?"

I have nothing to say, so she continues, "You disobeyed what I said. I would not have known you were missing if Caleb had not come back home. I called all the neighbors looking for you, but no one knew where you were. After your Big Daddy called the police, I remembered you asking about the Petersons' old home.

"I looked up their number in my phonebook even though that house has been empty for the past year. Fortunately for me, Sylvia answered the phone. She told me you were there and had been there a while. You and Tammi were napping, so I told her to wake you and send you home. That's how I knew to greet you at the brick wall."

I sat still in my chair, stiff as a board. I cannot believe what I am hearing. I think my mouth is wide open, but I am not sure because I am in a daze.

Big Daddy asks me a simple question. "Amilya Rose, what do you have to say for yourself?"

What can I say? I am busted. Summer vacation is just beginning, and I am already in trouble. All I can think about is the punishment I will have to face. I hate being grounded!

"Young lady, we are waiting," says Big Daddy.

"I'm sor—ry!" That's all I can say at the moment. The porch is so quiet that I could have heard a pin drop.

Finally, Big Momma speaks. "Amilya, we love you."

"Yes, ma'am, I know," I say.

"Your parents are trusting us to keep you safe. We all would have been devastated if something had happened to you."

"Yes, ma'am."

"I didn't tell you this, but I was planning to go up the street this afternoon to greet our new neighbors. I would have taken you and Caleb. However, as usual, you took it upon yourself to do the opposite of what I instructed you to do."

I can hear Big Daddy agreeing with what she is saying. Right when I am wondering if my parents know what I have done, Big Daddy says, "Just in case you are wondering, we have called your parents."

Oh no! "I don't want to go home. I want to stay with you all," I say. Huge tears begin to fall from my eyes. "I am so sorry. I should not have disobeyed you, Big Momma. I know I deserve to be punished, but please, please, please don't send me home!"

As I am pleading, I hope and pray that they listen to me. Going home would be horrible. I can handle being punished by my grandparents, but Mom and Dad would never let me see the light of day again!

"Amilya, stop all that crying," Big Momma says. She gives me her famous stare that means she knows I am overreacting.

Big Daddy says, "Your parents agreed to let you stay with us for now, but you better start thinking before you make decisions. I love you, baby, and I don't want you to ruin your summer vacation by being punished. Oh, and by the way, you are grounded for the next two weeks with no television or playtime."

I am shocked. There is nothing to do in the house for that long.

Before I can complain, Big Daddy says, "Your mom said you have some books you need to read for school, so you will read them over the next two weeks. Go to your bedroom now and think about what you have done. Your punishment starts today."

27

Reflection

I am glad it's bedtime. I walk slowly to my bedroom as tears drip from my eyes. Friends, I promise you my tears are real. The reality of what I have done has set in. I put on my bedclothes and lay in my bed, looking up at the ceiling and reflecting on my decisions.

The day started out just right, but it quickly turned into a sour apple. My adventure was flawed, as usual. While I am planning an adventure, I am so eager to do what I want that I don't stop to think about the consequences of my actions.

Deep down, I am truly sorry I lied to Aunt Sylvia and my grandparents. However, even though I am upset, I chuckle a little because I had fun with Tammi. Maybe I need to rethink going on adventures, but what is life without them?

I guess I should just change how I approach my adventures. For example, disappearing is serious. Someone could have really kidnapped me, and I might have been gone forever. I caused the police to respond to a false alarm, and I'm sure it took them away from a real crime. I also caused a ruckus in the neighborhood.

Summer vacation is just beginning, but my disappearing act has earned me two whole weeks of no playtime! I think about what can I do to make things right again. I suppose I will start by asking everyone involved to forgive me.

Next time, I will plan my adventure better by asking for permission to do what I want to do.

About the Author

Author Chavonne D. Stewart is a minister, missionary, writer, and blogger living in Atlanta, Georgia. Her blog, "Real Conversation 4 Real People," is an exploration of culture through conversation, without the restraints of political correctness. She is an executive board member of Sisters On Mission, Inc. Sisters On Mission's purpose is to educate, train, provide resources, and mobilize believers to increase their involvement in reaching the world for Christ. Chavonne holds an MS in Management from Troy University and a BA in History from Kennesaw State University. She enjoys history, DIY shows, traveling, reading, shopping, and spending time with family and friends.

Friends: Help Amilya Rose
reach her best friend Tammi
by choosing the right path
through the maze....Have Fun!!

The Adventures
of
Amilya Rose

Other Books by Chavonne Stewart

The Adventures of Amilya Rose: The Lie (December 2014)

24655662R00024

Made in the USA
Middletown, DE
01 October 2015